IS THERE A MONSTER IN MY CLOSET?

Written by
Johannah Gilman Paiva

Illustrated by
Paulette Rich Long

Color by
Jonas Fearon Bell

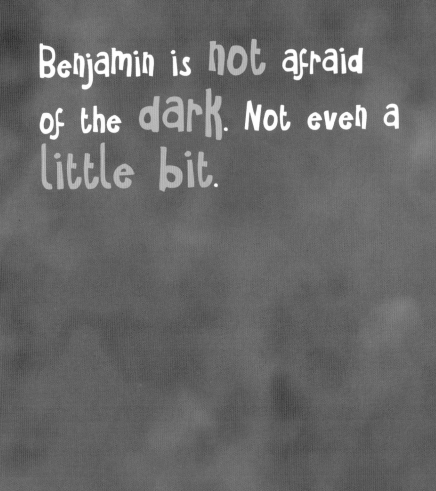

Benjamin is **not** afraid of the dark. Not even a little bit.

Every night, when it's time for bed, Benjamin puts on his pajamas, brushes his teeth, and climbs into bed without even checking underneath it. That's how brave he is.

Until one night, when
Benjamin was tucked
soundly in his bed, and a
BUMP woke him up.

"Who's there?"
Benjamin asked.

But no one answered.
"That's strange,"
thought Benjamin.
"Maybe I imagined it."

But then he heard it **again**, this time a bit louder: "BUMP!" Benjamin **jumped!**

"Isn't there anyone there?" Benjamin asked in his **bravest** voice, trying very hard not to be **scared**.

But again, **no one answered**.

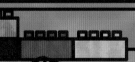

Benjamin scratched his head. "That's strange," he thought. "I'm sure this time I heard something."

So, Benjamin climbed out of his warm bed to see for himself what on Earth could be making that noise.

"Hellloooo?" called Benjamin, as he crept toward his closet door, which was open just a teeny bit. "Is anybody over here?" But, Benjamin didn't see anything in his closet, except for some of his toys, still sitting where he had left them.

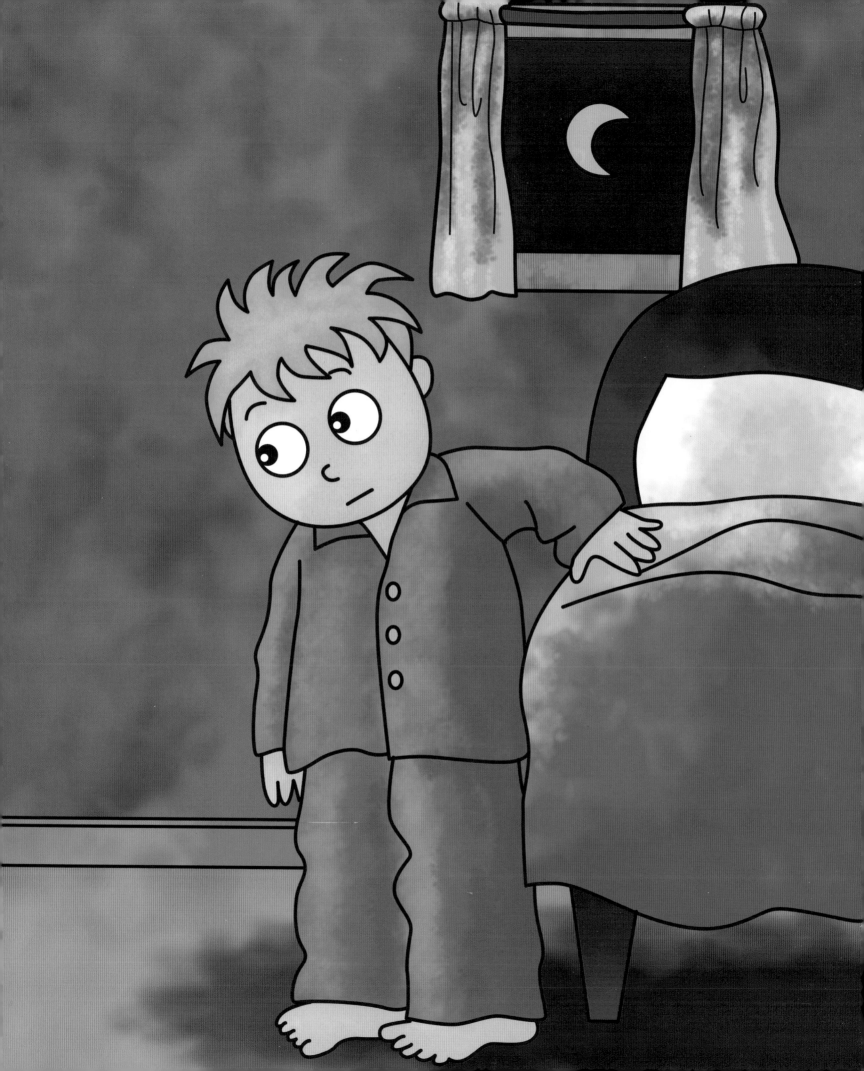

There was only **one** place left for Benjamin to check: under his bed. So, he **leapt** back onto his bed, **leaned** over the edge, and peeked under.

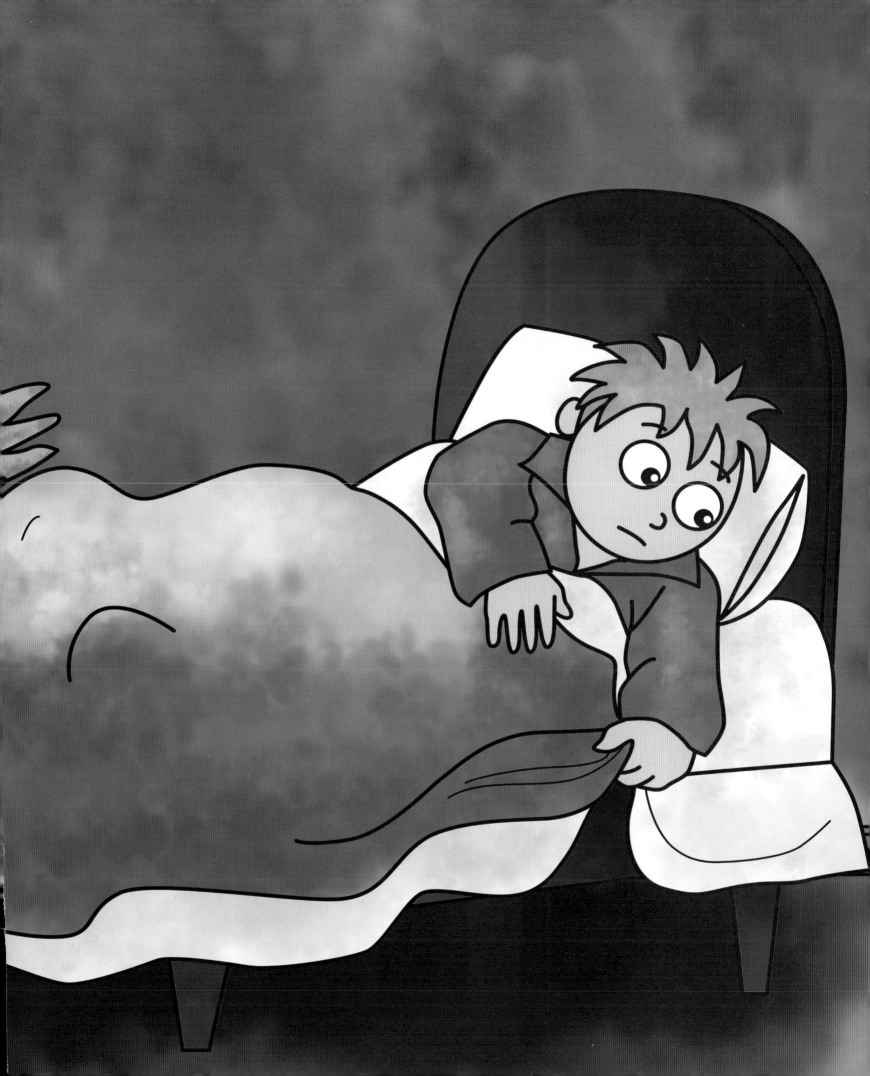

"Rex!" Benjamin cried, as his little dog hopped out from underneath the bed, licking Benjamin's cheek. "It was only you!" said Benjamin. "I KNEW there was nothing to be scared of!"

But just then, Benjamin heard another BUMP, this time with a little whimper as well. Benjamin turned around, and who was hiding behind his closet door, but three big, hairy, monsters, shaking with fright!

At first Benjamin felt **scared**, but then he saw that the monsters **looked even** more **scared** than he felt. "What's... what's wrong, monsters?" asked Benjamin, timidly.

"We are scared of the little monster you are holding! Will he bite us?!" they asked.

"Who, Rex?!" asked Benjamin.
"No! He's just my little dog! He wouldn't hurt anyone! Come over and see for yourselves!" The monsters crept closer. Rex did look friendly. They stopped shaking, and even began to smile a little bit.

"See!" said one monster friend to another. "I told you there was nothing to be afraid of!" Rex wagged his tail. Benjamin and Rex snuggled warmly in bed, and together they drifted off to sleep, with their new monster friends tucked snugly under the bed and in the closet.